CHILDREN IN THE HOLOCAUST

by Samantha S. Bell

FOCUS READERS

FOCUS READERS

www.focusreaders.com

Focus Readers is distributed by North Star Editions:
sales@northstareditions.com | 888-417-0195

Produced for Focus Readers by Red Line Editorial.

Content Consultant: Edward Snyder, Assistant Professor of History, Chowan University

Photographs ©: CAF pap/AP Images, cover, 1; dpa Dena/picture-alliance/dpa/AP Images, 4–5; Harris & Ewing/Harris & Ewing Collection/Library of Congress, 7; Fred Morley/Hulton Archive/Getty Images, 8–9; Everett Historical/Shutterstock Images, 11, 25; Red Line Editorial, 12; AP Images, 14–15, 19, 27, 39; New York World-Telegram and the Sun Newspaper Photograph Collection/Library of Congress, 17; Kaca Skokanova/Shutterstock Images, 21; Stanislaw Mucha/AP Images, 22–23; Imagno/Hulton Archive/Getty Images, 28–29; meunierd/Shutterstock Images, 31; Rainer Jensen/picture-alliance/dpa/AP Images, 32; Hulton Archive/Getty Images, 34–35; Franka Bruns/AP Images, 37; GiuseppeCrimeni/Shutterstock Images, 41; Byron H. Rollins/AP Images, 42–43

ISBN
978-1-63517-876-0 (hardcover)
978-1-63517-977-4 (paperback)
978-1-64185-180-0 (ebook pdf)
978-1-64185-079-7 (hosted ebook)

Library of Congress Control Number: 2018931698

Printed in the United States of America
Mankato, MN
April, 2019

ABOUT THE AUTHOR

Samantha S. Bell lives with her family in the upstate of South Carolina. She has a teaching degree in history and has written more than 75 nonfiction books for children.

TABLE OF CONTENTS

CHAPTER 1

HITLER'S HATRED

In the early 1930s, Germany was facing many hardships. Millions of people were out of work. Many Germans still felt angry about losing World War I (1914–1918). The German government was weak. As a result, the German people felt desperate for a change. Adolf Hitler and his Nazi party took advantage of this desperation.

Hitler was a powerful speaker. He spoke to large crowds, promising to solve Germany's problems.

Hitler had a variety of supporters, including many German youth.

In 1933, Hitler was appointed the head of the German government. Soon, the Nazis controlled Germany's economy, education, culture, and laws.

Hitler spoke of positive change. But in reality, he promoted **discrimination** and hate. Hitler and the Nazis believed that "**Aryans**" were superior to all others. Nazis hated people who did not look like them, especially Jews. Hitler blamed Jews for many of Germany's problems. Over the next few years, the Nazis created laws to take away Jewish people's freedoms. Jews could not own shops or be lawyers, teachers, or doctors. Jewish children could not attend school. Hitler's hatred for the Jews had no limits. Eventually, he would carry out plans to murder masses of European Jews.

Hitler wanted to expand the German empire. In 1939, Germany invaded Poland, causing the United Kingdom and France to declare war on

On September 1, 1939, news of the invasion of Poland spread across the world.

Germany. This was the beginning of World War II (1939–1945) in Europe.

From 1941 until the end of the war, the Nazi party **systematically** murdered millions of Jews. This mass murder of the Jewish people became known as the Holocaust. Many of the victims were children. They lost their homes, their parents, their families, and their lives.

CHAPTER 2

ESCAPE TO THE UNITED KINGDOM

Jack Adler was born in 1927 and grew up with his family in Berlin, Germany. After Jack's mother died in 1935, Jack's father struggled to take care of the family. He placed Jack and his siblings in a Jewish orphanage.

Meanwhile, the Nazis were gaining power in Germany. In 1933, they had begun building camps to hold political prisoners. The Nazis imprisoned anyone who opposed Hitler or the Nazi party.

Children seeking safety from the Nazis arrive in the United Kingdom in 1938.

The camps were called concentration camps because the prisoners were concentrated, or grouped closely, in one area. After the start of the war, the Nazis would open labor camps and, in 1941, death camps. They would use the death camps to gather and murder masses of Jews.

On the night of November 9, 1938, the Nazis violently attacked the Jews in Germany. They destroyed **synagogues** and killed dozens of Jews. They also took thousands of Jews to concentration camps. The incident became known as Kristallnacht, or the "Night of Broken Glass." During Kristallnacht, the orphanage that Jack lived in was set on fire. The children who lived there needed a new home.

After the attacks, the British government arranged for Jewish children in Germany to come to the United Kingdom. The children would

The windows of this Jewish-owned printing press were smashed on the Night of Broken Glass.

stay there until Germany was safe again. This effort was called Kindertransport, or "Children's Transport." Through the program, 11-year-old Jack would start a new life in the United Kingdom.

In March 1939, Jack and his siblings boarded trains with other children. They each had a bag with a few belongings and some food. Teachers and other adults also boarded the train. They accompanied the children on their trip.

Family members, including Jack's aunt and uncle, watched the trains depart. At the border, German police searched the children's bags. They did not allow the children to keep any valuables. The children continued to the Netherlands and then took a boat to the United Kingdom.

ROUTE TO SAFETY

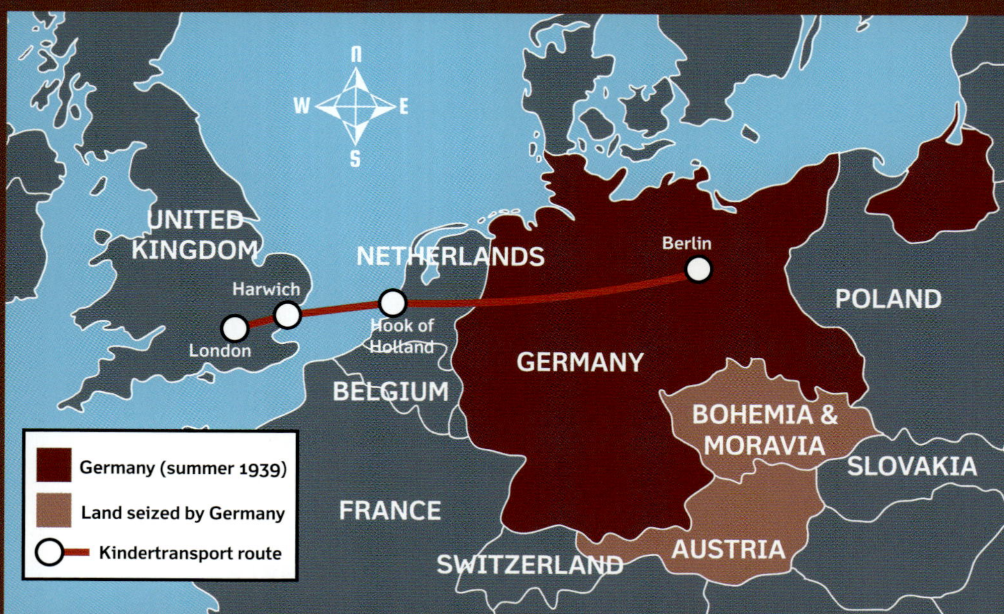

In London, England, Jack lived in a house with approximately 30 boys. When World War II broke out, the boys went to live with families in rural areas. Like the other children in the program, Jack attended a local school. But shortly before turning 14, Jack had to quit school to make money. He began work as an assistant to a jewelry maker.

Nearly 10,000 children escaped Nazi Germany through the Kindertransport program. But their lives were changed forever. Most of the children lost parents or other relatives during the war. After the war ended, some of the children stayed in the United Kingdom. Jack remained and earned a degree in mathematics. Others moved to the United States, Canada, Australia, or the new country of Israel. Their parents had saved them by sending them away. But many of the children never saw their parents again.

CHAPTER 3

TRAPPED IN GHETTOS

During World War II, the Nazis created hundreds of **ghettos** in Nazi-occupied areas. They used these ghettos to separate Jewish people from the rest of the population. Living conditions in the ghettos were so horrible that people died of starvation and disease. Children witnessed unimaginable violence. The Nazis shot and killed many people who lived in the ghettos.

German soldiers force a group of Jews to leave the Warsaw ghetto in 1943.

They sent others to concentration camps. Ed Herman was almost one of these victims.

Ed was born in Poland in 1931. He had a good home with two loving parents and a younger sister. When Ed was seven years old, his family went to visit his grandfather in Warsaw, Poland. Warsaw was an important center of Jewish culture and home to more than 350,000 Jews. As the Nazis advanced into Warsaw, Ed's father left to join the Polish Army. The rest of the family stayed behind.

In September 1939, the Polish Army in Warsaw surrendered to the Nazis. A year later, the Nazis formed a ghetto in the city. They forced more than 400,000 Jews into an area of 1.3 square miles (3.4 sq km). Jews had to wear armbands with the **Star of David** so they could be easily identified.

The Nazis sealed off the Warsaw ghetto from the rest of the city. They built a wall more than

Jewish residents of Warsaw could not go beyond the ghetto's tall concrete wall.

10 feet (3.0 m) high with barbed wire at the top. German guards surrounded it. Because so many people lived in the ghetto, several families had to share each apartment. Ed lived in a building with his grandfather. From his window, he saw the inside of the ghetto wall.

Like the others living in the ghetto, Ed always felt hungry. The Germans allowed the Jews to buy only small portions of bread and potatoes. Due to a flour shortage, some of Ed's bread contained sawdust. Fortunately, Ed's mother smuggled food into the ghetto for the family. She had light hair, so she was able to get a fake ID card as a so-called Aryan.

Winter in the ghetto was even more difficult. Shortages of heating fuel and warm clothes caused families to suffer in the cold. Many children lost their parents to disease. Older siblings were left to take care of their younger brothers and sisters.

Ed's mother knew that Ed had to leave if he was going to live. So in 1942, she smuggled Ed beyond the ghetto's walls and sent him out of the country. Ed escaped just in time. A few months

Nazis destroyed the Warsaw ghetto in 1943.

later, Nazis sent the remaining Jews in Warsaw to a concentration camp. Many of Ed's relatives did not survive. Later, Ed reunited with his mother, father, and sister.

MIRYAM L.

When Miryam L. was 10 years old, the Nazis sent her family to the Theresienstadt ghetto in Czechoslovakia. In **propaganda**, the Nazis called the ghetto a "spa town." They wanted people to think it was a safe place. They sent Jewish celebrities, Jewish veterans with disabilities, and older Jewish people to the ghetto. Eventually, many of them would be sent to death camps.

In 1944, the International Red Cross came to visit the ghetto. The Nazis prepared by painting houses and planting gardens. Later, Miryam spoke about the visit. "The beautiful children, especially my sister, were called, and they were taking pictures of them for how beautiful, how well-fed they looked," Miryam said. "I was like skin and bones. My glands were sticking out, and I was something horrible to look at."

The entrance to Theresienstadt carried the Nazi slogan "work will set you free."

Miryam's sister, Zora, died of illness when she was 14 years old. After Zora's death, Miryam's mother became depressed. "I would sometimes remind her . . . that I was still alive," Miryam recalled. "I kept telling her, 'I am here too, I am here!' and she didn't want to hear me." Despite the family's hardships, Miryam and her parents survived. On May 5, 1945, soldiers from the Soviet Union rescued them.

Esther V. L. and Miryam L. "A Tale of Terezin." *Our Stories.* World Federation of Jewish Child Survivors of the Holocaust and Descendants, 14 Dec. 2000. Web. 8 Mar. 2018.

CHAPTER 4

THE STRUGGLE FOR SURVIVAL

Before World War II, David Wolnerman lived with his family in Poland. His father died three months before Germany invaded the country. When the Nazis arrived, they threatened David's family. They told David he had to work in a camp if he wanted to save his family. He was only 13 years old when he went to the concentration camp at Auschwitz.

Auschwitz was the largest Nazi concentration camp complex.

The Nazis had begun sending families, including children, to concentration camps by the late 1930s. The Nazis established Auschwitz as a concentration camp in 1940. However, it soon became a complex of camps. By 1942, Auschwitz served as a concentration camp, labor camp, and death camp.

After arriving at Auschwitz, David stood in a line with other prisoners. A Nazi officer assessed each prisoner, telling them to go left or right. David noticed that old, young, and sick people went to the left line. When it was his turn, the Nazi officer asked his age. David said he was 18, and the officer sent him to the right.

Those in the left line were too young, old, or sick to work. They were eventually sent to a death camp. Here, innocent people faced torture and death. Nazis sent the prisoners into large rooms

German soldiers select and separate prisoners at a railway station at the Auschwitz concentration camp.

filled with a poisonous gas. More than one million people died in the gas chambers at Auschwitz.

Those in the right line were forced to perform hard labor. This included older children and children such as David who had lied about their age. These children worked long hours and suffered from disease and physical abuse. They did not know what was happening outside of the camp or even what day it was.

Throughout the war, the Nazis transferred David from camp to camp. He thought only of survival. At one point, he was lying sick on his wooden bunk without any food, water, or medicine. He thought he would never be free again.

Finally, in April 1945, US soldiers arrived at the Dachau concentration camp, where David was imprisoned. The soldiers **liberated** the camp and released the prisoners. At the time, David weighed only 80 pounds (36 kg). The US soldiers gave the prisoners food to eat, but the prisoners ate too much and became sick. Their digestive

THINK ABOUT IT

The children in the Holocaust experienced unforgettable acts of injustice. What do you think life was like for those who survived? How do you think they coped?

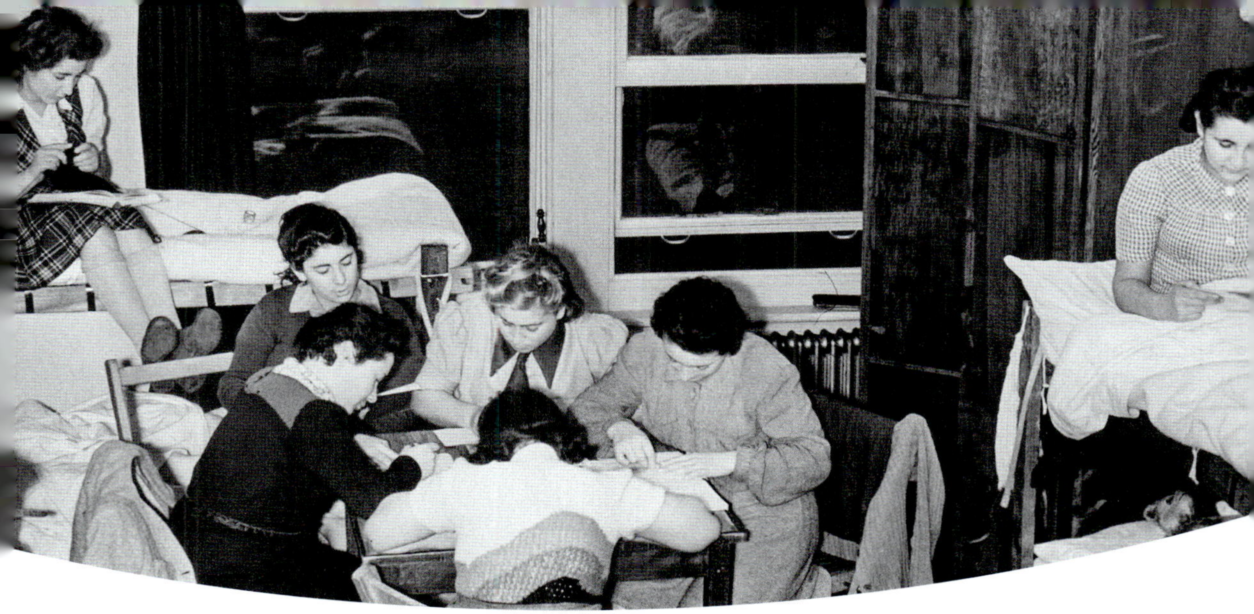

Young survivors recover at a youth home in England after being liberated from the Bergen-Belsen camp complex.

systems were not used to food. David then went to a **displaced** persons camp near Munich, Germany. Every day, Catholic nuns gave him breakfast. They started with only five spoons of oatmeal.

Although David survived, his mother, brother, and one of his sisters did not. They had died in concentration camps. Throughout the Holocaust, hundreds of thousands of Jews died in concentration camps. The Nazis murdered millions more in the death camps.

CHAPTER 5

THE FORGOTTEN VICTIMS

The Nazis targeted several groups of people in addition to Jews. One of the groups was the Roma, an ethnic group that originated in India. In Europe, some people thought the Roma came from Egypt. They incorrectly called the Roma "Gypsies." Many of the Roma did not fit into European society. Large groups of Roma often moved with the seasons. They also had different cultural practices from many other Europeans.

Nearly one million Roma lived in Europe before World War II.

In Europe, Roma faced discrimination due to their dark skin.

Ceija Stojka was born in 1933 into a large Roma family. Ceija's family traveled with other Roma families in wagons. They spent summers in the Austrian countryside. In the winter, they stayed in Vienna, the capital of Austria. During the winter of 1938, they parked at a campground. When the Nazis took over Austria in March, they told the Roma families they could not leave. Ceija's parents had to make their wagon into a wooden house.

After 1938, the Nazis widened their definition of Roma to include more people. According to the Nazis, a person was Roma if he or she had at least two great-grandparents who were part Roma. Their definition often included people who traveled without a home or had darker skin. The

A statue of a wagon in Kiev, Ukraine, stands as a memorial to the Roma killed in the Holocaust.

Nazis considered the Roma, in addition to Jews, to be an inferior race.

The Nazis built a fence around the campground where Ceija and her family lived. Police officers guarded the camp. When Ceija was eight years old, the Nazis took her father away and sent him to a concentration camp. Ceija never saw him again.

Ceija Stojka grew up to become a painter, writer, and musician.

The Nazis sent other Roma families to holding camps until they could be **deported**. In many of these camps, conditions were so bad that hundreds of people died. Similar to Jewish prisoners, the Roma were forced into labor camps and murdered in death camps. Nazis sent many Roma to the Auschwitz complex. When Ceija was 10 years old, her family was sent there as well.

Ceija nearly faced death upon her arrival at Auschwitz. However, when officers asked about

Ceija's age, Ceija's mother lied. She said Ceija was 16 years old and small for her age. The Nazis considered Ceija old enough to work, so they spared her life. Ceija later moved with her mother to the Ravensbrück camp and then the Bergen-Belsen camp.

The Nazis killed approximately 250,000 Roma during the Holocaust. Of the 200 members of Ceija's extended family, only Ceija, four of her siblings, and her mother survived. In 1945, the British liberated the Bergen-Belsen camp. Ceija and her family were finally free.

THINK ABOUT IT

The Nazis also targeted certain religious groups, people who were gay, and people with disabilities. How do you think they or their families may have felt? Do these individuals still suffer discrimination today?

victoria

CHAPTER 6

SAFE IN SECRET

Some Jewish families went into hiding to avoid concentration camps. Other families sent their children away to hide. The decision to go into hiding was not an easy one. Families had to find someone willing to take the risk of hiding them. Many times, they had to pay for the hiding place. Children who went into hiding often lived in secret rooms in homes of strangers. If the Nazis found them, they would face severe punishment.

Jews in hiding often lived in small, cramped spaces such as cellars.

In 1942, eight-year-old Floris K. had to leave her home in Belgium. Nazis had taken over the city where she lived and started deporting Jews. Floris's mother sent Floris and her sister to a children's home that housed more than 50 children. When Floris's mother found out that many of the children were Jewish, she decided to find a safer place. She knew the Nazis would likely target the children's home.

Some children in hiding could not go outside. They stayed in cellars, attics, barns, and chicken coops, where they had to remain quiet. Those who had lighter skin could go to school. Children on farms helped with chores, and those in the cities worked in factories.

Sometimes, the people who took in the children did not take good care of them. They only wanted money. Floris's second hiding place housed eight

The small closet (left) in this Berlin home served as a hiding place for Jews.

other Jewish children. They had nothing to do all day, and they often went hungry. The father of the house talked about Nazis to frighten them.

Floris liked her third hiding place much better. She moved in with a family that included grandparents, parents, and three children. They made her feel welcome. Because Floris could not go to school, she spent the days reading books from the family's huge collection.

When it was no longer safe for her to stay there, Floris moved to a house with six adults, including her parents. Every day, they practiced racing to the secret closet under the staircase in case the Nazis came. Although Floris was with her parents, she lived in constant fear.

In her next two hiding places, Floris stayed with women who lived alone. Like many of the caregivers, the women did not show Floris any affection. Floris often felt extremely lonely. Fortunately, her last hiding place was with a kind woman and her elderly father. Floris stayed there

THINK ABOUT IT

Many children in hiding knew that Nazis could find them at any moment. What do you think it was like to live in fear? What other emotions might children have felt?

A Polish family emerges from hiding in September 1944.

only three months before the war ended. She had moved six times in two years.

Historians are not sure how many children survived the Holocaust in hiding. Some children, like Floris, returned home to their families after the war. Others no longer had families. And some stayed with their caregivers. All were victims of the Holocaust.

ANNE FRANK

In July 1942, 13-year-old Anne Frank and her family went into hiding. Four other people hid with them. They stayed in the extra rooms above her father's office in Amsterdam, the capital of the Netherlands.

Anne took along a diary her parents had given her for her birthday. She thought of the diary as a friend. Writing about her experience helped her cope with her new life.

While in hiding, Anne's family stayed inside and remained quiet. The only fresh air came through a small window in the attic. Anne wrote, "Not being able to go outside upsets me more than I can say, and I'm terrified our hiding place will be discovered and that we'll be shot." Like others in hiding, Anne and her family were always afraid.

After more than a year of hiding, Anne wrote about what she missed from her old life. "Most of

A picture of Anne Frank writing at her desk stands on display at the US Holocaust Memorial Museum.

all, I long to have a home of our own, to be able to move around freely and have someone help me with my homework again, at last," she wrote. "In other words, to go back to school!"

In August 1944, the Nazi secret police found Anne's family and sent them to concentration camps. Anne and her sister died of illness at the Bergen-Belsen camp just a couple months before the camp was liberated.

Anne Frank. *The Diary of a Young Girl*. New York: Alfred A. Knopf, 2010. Print. 30, 97.

CHAPTER 7

THE SEARCH FOR FAMILY

On May 8, 1945, Germany surrendered to the **Allied Forces**, ending World War II in Europe. Hitler had committed suicide only one week earlier. The Nazi officials eventually went on trial for their horrible crimes. However, the lives of the children who survived the Holocaust would never be the same.

In the final stages of the war, Soviet soldiers had begun liberating the concentration camps.

Prisoners of the Buchenwald concentration camp walk to a hospital after liberation by the US Army.

Troops from the United States, Canada, France, and the United Kingdom also freed prisoners from the camps. Most of the children went to orphanages or children's homes. Only a small percentage reunited with their parents.

Surviving Roma children faced many hardships. The Roma had no country to flee to. In many

MAJOR EVENTS OF THE HOLOCAUST

1933 – 1945

JANUARY 1933
Adolf Hitler is elected chancellor of Germany.

MARCH 1933
The Nazis open the first concentration camps.

NOVEMBER 1938
The Nazis attack German Jews during Kristallnacht.

SEPTEMBER 1939
Germany invades Poland, starting World War II.

NOVEMBER 1940
The Nazis establish the Warsaw ghetto.

DECEMBER 1941
The Nazis use the first gas chambers to commit mass murder at the Chelmno death camp.

JULY 1944
Majdanek becomes the first concentration camp liberated by the Soviet Union.

MAY 1945
Germany surrenders, ending World War II in Europe.

cases, they lost everything they had owned. Nazis had burned their wagons and shot their horses. No organizations helped the Roma restart their lives. Many people still thought Roma were criminals.

Children who had been in hiding went in search of their parents. However, many of their families had died. Parents who had survived spent months searching for their children. Some children had been very young when they went into hiding and did not remember their parents. Some loved their adopted families and did not want to return home.

Many survivors of the Holocaust wrote down their experiences. The stories of survivors honor the victims and the people who risked their lives to help them. By sharing their stories, survivors remind the world of the tragedies that took place. And by remembering, people hope to prevent such injustices from happening again.

FOCUS ON

CHILDREN IN THE HOLOCAUST

Write your answers on a separate piece of paper.

1. Write a letter to a friend describing what you learned about children in the Holocaust.

2. Do you think children in hiding should have remained with their adopted families or returned home? Why?

3. Which year did Kristallnacht take place?

A. 1927
B. 1938
C. 1940

4. Why did David Wolnerman lie about his age to the Nazi officer?

A. The younger children were forced to perform hard labor.
B. People 18 years and older were allowed to leave the camp.
C. The younger children were more likely to be killed.

Answer key on page 48.

GLOSSARY

Allied Forces
The victorious countries of World War II, including the Soviet Union, the United Kingdom, France, and the United States.

Aryans
A racial term that Nazis inaccurately used to describe non-Jewish white people of German or Northern European descent.

deported
Forced to leave a country.

discrimination
Unfair treatment of others based on who they are or how they look.

displaced
Forced to leave one's home, usually because of war or other dangers.

ghettos
Parts of a city usually closed off by a wall or fence.

liberated
Freed from the control of enemy forces.

propaganda
False information used to promote a particular political cause or leader.

Star of David
A six-pointed star that symbolizes the Jewish people and Israel.

synagogues
Buildings used for Jewish religious services.

systematically
Following a fixed plan or system.

TO LEARN MORE

BOOKS

Golabek, Mona, and Lee Cohen. *The Children of Willesden Lane: A True Story of Hope and Survival during World War II.* New York: Little, Brown and Company, 2017.

Leyson, Leon. *The Boy on the Wooden Box: How the Impossible Became Possible . . . on Schindler's List.* New York: Atheneum Books for Young Readers, 2013.

Steele, Philip. *The Holocaust: The Origins, Events, and Remarkable Tales of Survival.* New York: Scholastic, 2016.

NOTE TO EDUCATORS

Visit **www.focusreaders.com** to find lesson plans, activities, links, and other resources related to this title.

INDEX

Answer Key: 1. Answers will vary; **2.** Answers will vary; **3.** B; **4.** C